I'm Reading About

MISSISSIPPI

The Magnolia State!

GALLOPADE

by Carole Marsh

Printed and Manufactured in Peachtree City, GA., USA
www.gallopade.com

Book design: John Hanson

Editorial manager: Janice Baker

Mississippi is a great state.

It is one of a kind.

What makes Mississippi special?

Let's read about it and see!

NATIVE AMERICANS

Who lived in Mississippi first?

Native Americans did!

They moved around to find food.
They hunted in Mississippi's woods.
They fished in Mississippi's rivers.
They gathered fruits and seeds and nuts.

EXPLORERS

The first explorers came to Mississippi in 1540.
They came from the country of Spain.

Hernando de Soto was their leader.
He and his men were looking for cities of gold!

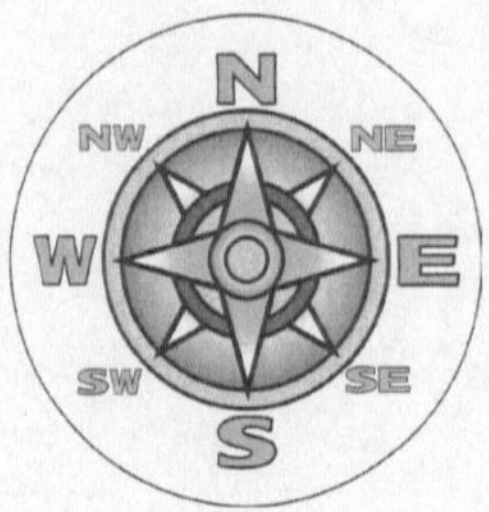

SETTLEMENT

A man named Pierre Le Moyne d'Iberville came from France to America. He started the first settlement in Mississippi. He named it Fort Maurepas.

Fort Maurepas was built where Ocean Springs is today!

FORT MAUREPAS
(1699–1702)
Fort Maurepas
OCEAN SPRINGS
Site of Ft. Maurepas &
Old Biloxi, founded 1699
by Iberville. Louisian
capital to 1702 & fro
1719 to 1720 when capit
was removed to Ft. Louis,
present site of Biloxi.
Fort Maurepas

STATEHOOD

Mississippi was the 20th state to join the United States of America!

Isn't it great,
to be a state!
I bet Mississippi
could hardly wait!

Mississippi became a state in 1817.

Mississippi
The 20th State
Here we are!

FLAG

I am the state flag.
I was adopted in 2021.

What colors am I?
Red. White. Blue. Gold.

Count my stars.
Count my stripes.

Look at me.
What else do you see?

IN GOD WE TRUST

CAPITAL

Say hello to Jackson,
the capital city of Mississippi!

There is an important building in Jackson.
It is the State Capitol.
Mississippi's laws are made there!

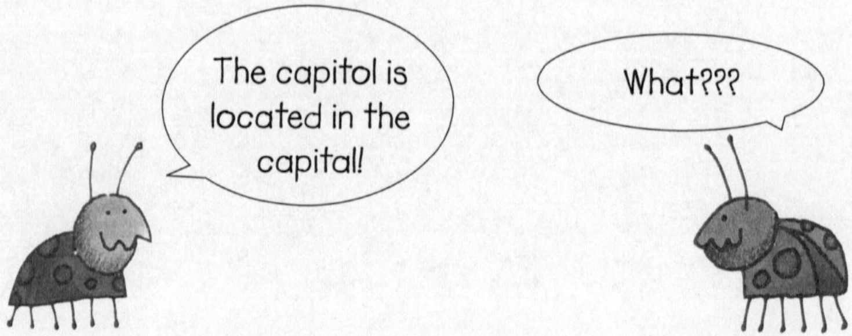

Capitol
Jackson
Capital

SEAL

I am a seal,
but I am not the State Seal.
If I were, I would be very important.
I would be stamped on many official papers.
(Ouch, that might hurt!)

THE GREAT SEAL OF THE STATE OF MISSISSIPPI
IN GOD WE TRUST

Now, that's official!

NICKNAME

State nicknames are fun!
State nicknames are great!
They share fun facts
about each state!

Mississippi's nickname is "The Magnolia State."

Magnolia flowers have a lovely scent!

The Magnolia State

BORDERS

Look at Mississippi.
Mississippi is in a region called "the South."

Mississippi borders four other states.
Find them on the map!

Borders

TENNESSEE
ARKANSAS
MISSISSIPPI
ALABAMA
LOUISIANA
GULF OF MEXICO
Howdy, neighbors!

COUNTIES

Mississippi is divided into 82 counties.
Counties are a form of local government.

Counties provide services that people need!
Those services include:

Schools **Parks** **Libraries** **Police** **Firefighters** **and More!**

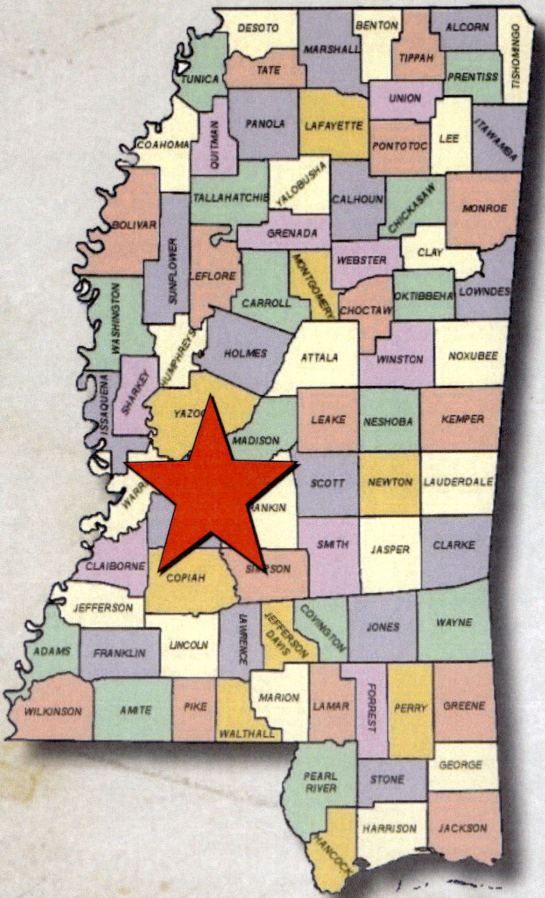

Counties

MISSISSIPPI'S CAPITAL, JACKSON, IS THE COUNTY SEAT OF HINDS COUNTY.

PEOPLE

Many famous people

William Faulkner

Famous author who wrote books about life in the South

B.B. King

Musician known as "The King of the Blues"

Elvis Presley

Musician known as "The King of Rock and Roll"

call our state home!

Let's hang out!

PEOPLE

Oprah Winfrey

Television talk show host

Ruby Bridges

First black child to attend an all-white elementary school in the South

Jim Henson

Puppeteer and creator of The Muppets

Mockingbird

I am the state bird, and I fly
over Mississippi, proud and high.

As I fly, up in the sky,
I flap my wings to tell you "Hi!"

The Mississippi state bird is the Mockingbird.

BIRD

Magnolia

FLOWER

I am the Magnolia.
I am the state flower.

I grow where it's warm and sunny.
I bloom in spring and summer.
I help make Mississippi beautiful!

Look at me! Smell me!
I bloom on the Magnolia tree.

Magnolia

T
R
E
E

I am a Magnolia—I'm the state tree.
All over Mississippi is where to find me.

My roots run deep, they keep me strong.
My leaves stay green, all year long.

I stand up straight, big and tall.
Don't climb too high—it would hurt to fall!

Honeybee

I am the Honeybee.
I am the state insect.

I might sting you if you bother me,
But really, I am your friend.

I carry pollen from flower to flower.
I make honey.
I help Mississippi crops grow.

BZZZZZZZZZZZZ!

INSECT

Gulf of Mexico

BEACHES

Let's go to the beach!

We can swim in the waves.
We can play in the sand.

We can build a big castle
where water meets land.

Mississippi's beaches are home to many animals:

Sea Turtles **Fish** **Birds** **Crabs** **Dolphins** **and More!**

Forests

FORESTS

Mississippi's forests are the place to be.
Hiking, fishing, camping—
fun for you and me.

Under the shade
of the tall trees,
you can see all the beautiful leaves!

Rivers

RIVERS

Mississippi has many rivers.
People like to use rivers for boating and fishing!

This habitat is home to many animals:

Birds **Deer** **Snakes** **Frogs** **Fish** **and More!**

Mississippi's first explorers traveled along the Mississippi River!

Vicksburg National Military Park

LANDMARK

Vicksburg National Military Park
is in Vicksburg, Mississippi.

The park was built to remember
the Battle of Vicksburg.
It was a major battle in the Civil War.
Many brave soldiers fought at Vicksburg.

Vicksburg is located along
the Mississippi River.

Mississippi Crops

cotton

Soybeans

Rice

corn

AGRICULTURE

Mississippi has many farms.
Why?
Because Mississippi has good soil and a warm climate!

Some of the top crops grown in Mississippi are:

Cotton **Soybeans** **Rice** **Corn**

Hey!
Don't forget about me!
I am a young chicken.
They call me a "broiler."
Mississippi raises lots of broilers!

Sports in Mississippi

SPORTS

Baseball! Basketball! Football!
Mississippi has it all.

Whether you like to watch or play,
You are sure to have a ball!

Rebels **Bulldogs**

Golden Eagles

& More!

Mississippi: Home of the Mississippi River

CLAIM TO FAME

The Mississippi River runs along the west side of Mississippi. It is the second-longest river in the United States! It runs from Minnesota to the Gulf of Mexico!

Steamboats used to travel up and down the Mississippi River. It was like a big highway in the middle of the United States!

GLOSSARY

climate: weather conditions in an area over a long period of time

habitat: a place where plants or animals naturally live

laws: rules made by the government

pollen: a yellow powder that helps plants make new plants

puppeteer: a person who works with puppets

region: an area that has similar characteristics

settlement: the first community in an area

steamboat: a boat that moves by steam power